KLOOZ

Stage
Fright

by J. Banscherus

translated by Ann Berge

illustrated by Ralf Butschkow

STONE ARCH BOOKS
a capstone imprint

First published in the United States in 2011
by Stone Arch Books
A Capstone Imprint
151 Good Counsel Drive, P.O. Box 669
Mankato, Minnesota 56002
www.capstonepub.com

First published by Arena Verlag GmbH
Würzburg, Germany
Original title: *Ein Fall für Kwiatkowski – Monster, Mond und Mottenpulver*

Copyright © 2009 Jürgen Banscherus
Illustrations copyright © 2009 Ralf Butschkow

*Library of Congress Cataloging-in-Publication Data is available on the
Library of Congress website.*

Library binding: 978-1-4342-2129-2

Graphic Designer: Kay Fraser
Production Specialist: Michelle Biedscheid

Table of Contents

KLOOZ
Stage
Fright

TOP SECRET

CHAPTER 1

I Took the Case

There are thirteen other private detectives in this town besides me. Those guys in the dark sunglasses and old shoes take cases about disappearing husbands, stolen inventions, and international crooks. Me? I like my cases a little bit smaller.

That's why, up until now, I've been able to solve every case I've taken. Other detectives can only dream of having such a perfect record.

There are weird things about every private detective. For instance, one guy I know never takes off his crumpled detective hat, even when he's sleeping. Another one doesn't carry a weapon, but he never leaves the house without a lollipop. And a third uses so many wigs and fake beards that sometimes he doesn't even remember who he's supposed to be.

My weird things are my gum, Carpenter's Chewing Gum, which I'm almost constantly chewing, and my cap. I only take it off when I absolutely have to, like in the shower or when I'm getting my hair cut.

Some people make fun of me for the gum and the cap. But I don't really care what they say.

I need my gum to think. And my baseball cap with the big "K" on it keeps my brain going at just the right temperature.

All private eyes have rules about their cases, too. One guy, for example, never deals with the number 13. It brings bad luck.

Another detective I know won't take a case if the police are also involved. And another one never takes a case if he has to use a wheelchair.

For me, there are only two rules: never look for a lost pet, and never take a case from a teacher.

But sometimes you have to do something you really don't want to do. Like my last case, for example.

A few weeks ago, my school celebrated its 100th anniversary.

The highlight of the big party was the play that our theater club had been practicing since the beginning of the school year. Mrs. Linden wrote the play and was also the director. She teaches first grade.

About a month ago, she came to see me during recess. I was sitting on a little wall near the trash bins and eating my lunch. Mom had loaded my sandwich sky-high with salami, cheese, and pickle slices. I had to open my mouth almost to my ears so that I could bite into it.

"Klooz?" asked Mrs. Linden.

I nodded. Mom told me never to speak with my mouth full. And I obey this rule.

"Mr. Konzelmann told me you work as a detective," Mrs. Linden continued.

I nodded again. Mr. Konzelmann is my teacher. Unfortunately, he wouldn't know a joke if it bit him. But other than that, he's fine.

"I need your help," she said.

"No way," I replied, after I swallowed.

"No way? Why?" she asked.

"At school, I'm a student, not a detective," I answered. "I don't mix jobs."

She smiled. "Mr. Konzelmann told me that you're one of his very best students," she said.

I wasn't sure if I should believe her or not.

Mr. Konzelmann had never praised me like that. He'd never even said anything to my mother.

I stayed strong. "I never take a case from a teacher," I said.

She smiled again. "I can understand that," she said. "But first, don't you want to hear what it's about?"

I looked down at my watch. We still had a little time until recess was over. And besides, I'm always curious about new jobs. "All right, fire away!" I said.

It seemed Mrs. Linden was having trouble with the rehearsals for the play, "Trip to the Moon." One of the highlights of the play was when the star actor disappeared into the basement through a trap door on the stage.

Every time they practiced this scene, the star would quit the show! They were already on their fourth actor!

"Did they hurt themselves?" I wanted to know.

She shook her head. "No, they were fine."

"Then your actors must be scared to fall through the stage," I said.

Again, she shook her head. "The boys fought over this role, and it was because of that scene! They thought the disappearance would be cool."

I thought for a moment. "What did they say once they were back on stage?"

"That they didn't want to be in the play anymore," she told me.

"Nothing else?" I asked.

"Nothing else," she said.

"How did they look?" I asked.

"Pale," answered Mrs. Linden. "Yes, they were all suddenly very pale."

"Did they have any injuries? On their heads, for example?" I asked, thinking over the possibilities.

"No, there was nothing," Mrs. Linden said. "Absolutely nothing! No injuries at all! I checked!"

We were silent for a minute.

Mrs. Linden was new to our school last year, and I didn't know a whole lot about her. But with her long black hair and blue eyes, she looked kind of dangerous.

Like a spy, for example, or an undercover agent.

"Who were the star actors?" I asked, going back to my questioning.

"The first actor was Greg Hartman from fourth grade," Mrs. Linden said.

"Who was second?" I asked.

"The second actor to play the part was a boy named Larry Stindle, from the third grade," she told me.

"Got it. And who was the third actor?" I asked her.

"That was Sebastian Buck. Isn't he in your class?" she said.

Sebastian?

The boy who wanted to be a bomber pilot?

The boy who was never scared, even when we took a field trip to a farm and he came face-to-face with a full-grown bull?

If Sebastian had given up the starring role, there must be something crazy going on.

Before I could ask any more questions, the bell rang.

"So what do you think?" asked Mrs. Linden.

I could tell that she already knew the answer. Maybe she really had worked as a secret agent in her last career.

"I'll take the case," I said.

"And what kind of payment do you want?" she asked.

"The usual," I said.

She frowned. Didn't she know my payment?

"Five packs of Carpenter's Chewing Gum," I explained. "Mr. Konzelmann can tell you where to get them."

CHAPTER 2

Bravest Kid in School

I knew exactly what to do.

First, I'd have to talk to Greg, Larry, and Sebastian.

Then I'd investigate the basement of the theater.

Finally, I'd be on the lookout during a rehearsal and watch what happened to the star actor after the disappearance scene. Then I'd know exactly what was going on.

For dinner, my mom had cooked goulash. The brown goop was not exactly one of my favorite dishes. Luckily, there was lemon ice cream for dessert.

"How was school?" Mom asked as she drank her coffee.

She never asked this question before we ate. She probably didn't want to spoil our appetites. Every once in a while, I had to tell her about my not-so-good grades.

"Just fine," I answered.

"Do you have a new case?" she wanted to know.

I nodded. "Something's fishy in our theater club. They're rehearsing a play for the school anniversary. Mrs. Linden wants me to find out what's wrong. She's the director."

"So nothing dangerous?" Mom asked.

"I don't think so," I told her.

"You'll figure it out," she said, as she gathered the dishes.

After dinner, I looked in the phone book and found the addresses of the three star actors.

But before I visited them, I went to see my oldest and best friend, Olga. I needed a new pack of Carpenter's Chewing Gum, and Olga's newsstand was on my way.

Silently, she slid me a pack of gum over the counter. Right away, I popped a piece of the good stuff between my teeth.

"What's wrong, Olga?" I asked, as my teeth danced up and down with joy.

"Toothache," she mumbled.

"You should brush your teeth more often!" I told her.

She grimaced. "I do, Klooz! I brush my teeth morning, noon, and night! But when your wisdom tooth bothers you, you can't do a darn thing!"

"Then go to the dentist to get it pulled," I said.

"I'm scared," she whispered, after taking a deep breath.

"Should we go together?" I offered.

She shook her head. "I can do it by myself," she answered.

Suddenly, something important occurred to me. "Do you know anyone at the theater?" I asked. Then I noticed that Olga's right cheek was much fatter than the left. The poor woman must have really been in pain.

OW!

"Well, there's Old Karl," she mumbled. "He's been buying papers from me for the past thirty years."

"What does he do at the theater?" I asked.

"He has something to do with the costumes," she told me. I wrote Karl's name down and said goodbye to Olga.

Usually, Olga would say, "Bye, my angel!" or "See you later, sweetie!" But that day, she didn't say a word. I could have kissed her for that.

At Greg's, I had to wait a while for him to open the door. He looked a little tired, and his shirt wasn't tucked into his pants.

"What are you doing here, Klooz?" he asked, shocked.

"You were the star actor in the play," I said.

He nodded.

"Why did you quit?" I asked.

"Why do you care?" Greg asked.

"I just want to know," I answered.

"I just wasn't interested anymore," he said.

"And what was in the theater basement?" I asked.

He paused for a second. "Nothing," he answered. "Absolutely nothing. Bye."

On the way to Larry's house, thoughts flew through my head like bouncing balls. Greg didn't tell me everything, that was for sure. But why not? Was he scared? Was he being threatened? Were we being watched? Did he know?

I tried to figure everything out.

Larry was only in third grade, but he towered over me by more than half a head. "What do you want?" he asked. "I have to go to my piano lesson."

I tried to be sneakier with my questions, but Larry said the same thing Greg had. He told me he just wasn't interested in playing the role anymore. He also said there wasn't anything in the theater basement.

You didn't have to be a detective to figure out that the two boys had spoken to each other. Maybe Greg called Larry after I went to see him.

Sebastian's mother brought me right to her son's room. There he was, among piles and piles of notebooks and books, pants, shirts, comics, and his computer. "Want to play?" he asked me without looking up.

"No time," I answered. "Mrs. Linden wants me to play the lead role in 'Trip to the Moon,'" I added.

"Got it! Another point!" came the sounds from behind the computer. It seemed like Sebastian wasn't even listening to me. Then he got up from his desk.

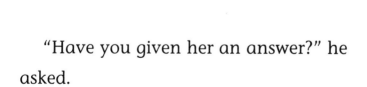

"Have you given her an answer?" he asked.

I shook my head.

"Don't do it," he told me.

"Why not?" I asked.

"Because . . ." Sebastian hesitated. "Because the play is dumb. And because Mrs. Linden is dumb. And because everyone else in the play is dumb," he said quickly.

"What's with the theater basement?" I asked.

Sebastian shot up. "W . . . w . . . with the basement?" he stuttered. "Nothing's with the basement!"

"What are you afraid of, Sebastian?" I asked.

His eyes narrowed. "Afraid?" he screamed angrily. "Are you crazy?"

I took my time on the way home.

It had begun to rain, and soon my hair was stuck to my forehead. I didn't notice. The solution to the puzzle was in the basement of that theater. I'd bet my last piece of gum on it.

That night, I went to bed early, even though I wasn't tired. In order to crack the case of what was scaring even Sebastian, the bravest kid in my class, I'd need plenty of rest.

CHAPTER 3

The Trap Door

The next morning, my mom had to shake me until I finally woke up. I looked at my watch. I had slept twelve hours.

"I have to go to a meeting at the hospital this afternoon," Mom said at breakfast.

That was perfect. I could start my investigation of the theater right after school.

"When will you be back?" I asked.

"By dinner at the latest. And pay attention at school, okay?" she said.

How could I? I had much more important things to do. My detective work would have to come first.

School was barely over before I made my way over to the theater.

There were cashiers at both ticket counters in the lobby. In front of one of them stood two old men.

The cashier next to them had red hair, wore lots of makeup, and was trimming her long fingernails as she waited for the customers.

"Is Karl around?" I asked her.

She placed the nail clippers on a towel in the ticket booth. "Do you mean Old Karl?" she asked.

"Yes," I said.

"Just a moment." She picked up the telephone and dialed a number. "There's a kid here to see you," she said. "What's your name?" she asked me.

"Klooz," I told her.

"His name is Klooz," she said into the phone.

"Karl is downstairs," she said, after she hung up. "Take the stairs on the left. Go through the door to the basement. Karl's waiting for you down there."

I opened a piece of Carpenter's and took off.

The door to the basement creaked loudly as I opened it. There was a man waiting for me there in the barely lit hallway.

He wasn't much taller than I was. He was wearing a black cap and a blue shirt. His eyes were hidden behind dark sunglasses.

"What do you want from me?" asked a powerful voice that couldn't possibly belong to his tiny body.

"Are you Karl?" I asked.

The man nodded.

"I'm Klooz, private —"

"Detective, I know," Karl interrupted me. "Olga told me all about it."

After walking through a maze of hallways, we came to a room with a desk, two stools, a small workbench, and an old telephone. Old, yellowing theater posters hung on the walls.

"What can I do for you?" he asked.

Did his voice sound unsure, or was it just me?

I explained to Karl what Mrs. Linden had told me.

"I bet you want to get a look at what's directly under the stage," he said when I was finished. "The scene of the crime."

"Exactly," I said.

"Should I bring you there?" he asked.

"If you don't mind, yes, please," I said politely.

First he showed me the room that Greg, Larry, and Karl had disappeared into. Above us, there was a trap door. On the ground in front of us were piles and piles of foam mattresses.

"Do you want to try it?" asked Karl. I nodded.

I climbed a ladder up to the trap door and opened it. The next thing I knew, I found myself standing on a big, dark stage.

"Just fall backward very slowly," said Karl.

"Backward?" I repeated.

"Don't be scared," he answered. "Nothing will happen to you."

I stood on the very edge of the square hole in the stage. Then I took a deep breath and let myself fall. With a soft plop, I landed safely on the pile of mattresses.

No, it couldn't have been that fall that made Sebastian and the others quit the role. No way. Falling was fun. I could understand why those three had fought over the role.

"Everything okay?" asked Karl, as he closed the trap door.

"Of course," I said. "Now, how did the boys get back to the stage?"

Karl waved for me to follow him. First we passed a closet packed with colorful costumes.

Then we walked through many rooms with bits and pieces of old sets.

There were staircases, ancient archways, huge dragons made from paper, and wooden ramps that any skateboarder would get excited about.

Finally, we entered a room with a huge sink and empty hangers. "This is where the actors change," explained Karl.

"And what's in there?" I asked, pointing to a red door with "Keep Out" painted on it.

"Well . . ." said Karl. He scratched the back of his head.

"May I open it and see?" I asked.

Karl shook his head. "I don't have a key for that room," he told me.

Then he opened the door we had just come through, the one that led back upstairs and out of the basement. "Over there, to the left, is the way to the stage. Bye, Klooz. I have to get back to work," he said.

I thanked him and then asked, "Are you here during rehearsals for 'Trip to the Moon?'"

"Always," he said.

"Has anything strange been happening?" I asked.

He hesitated a second. "No. Nothing." Then he turned and hurried away.

In front of the theater, I almost crashed into Mrs. Linden. "Why, hello there, Klooz!" she said. Then she asked about my investigation.

"It's going well so far," I answered. "Have you found a new actor?"

"Yes," she told me. "Mario Schulte from the fourth grade. Nobody wanted to do it but him."

CHAPTER 4

The Mother and the Monster

Now all that was left was the last part of my investigation. At least I hoped I was almost done.

I found a hiding spot in the basement of the theater and watched as Mario let himself fall through the trap twice. Every time, he landed safely on the mattresses, went back up to the stage, and continued acting.

Well, "acting" wasn't exactly the right word.

He stood on stage like a refrigerator on two legs, forgot his lines, and mumbled like he had some teeth missing. Mrs. Linden didn't seem happy.

Because I couldn't think of anything else to do, I asked Karl to let me look around the basement one more time.

"So?" he asked when I was finished. "Did you find anything?"

I shook my head.

"You can't always be lucky," he said, and returned to the red velvet costume he was sewing up.

I waited at the end of the rehearsal near the actors' entrance. I would never solve this case if there wasn't anything to solve. Maybe Greg, Larry, and Sebastian just didn't want to be in the play anymore.

Mrs. Linden left the theater. "This play is a flop!" she said sadly.

I nodded. Mario was the worst actor of all time. Then I said, "That's it for me. I'm sorry, but I can't help you, Mrs. Linden." I didn't tell her that it was the first case I wasn't able to solve.

"But what if you take over the lead role?" she asked. "Please, Klooz!"

"Forget it!" I answered. "Not even if wild horses dragged me on stage!"

That night, I couldn't sleep. Not even Carpenter's Chewing Gum could help me now.

The longer I thought about it, the more I was suspicious about that locked red door I had seen in the theater basement. I had the feeling that I had seen something in that theater that was important to the case.

I couldn't help thinking about the people that had to do with the case. There wasn't anything weird about Greg or Larry. Sebastian seemed scared of something, but other than that, he was fine. Mario was a bad actor, but that wasn't anything suspicious. Karl was suspicious, but nothing remarkable. Mrs. Linden was normal. The cashier woman . . .

I sat up when I thought of her. Red hair, nice dress, a friendly laugh, and a nametag on her jacket! "Christiane Schulte," it said.

Mario's last name was Schulte. What if the cashier was Mario's mother? What if she wanted her son to get the starring role? What if Karl had helped get rid of the other actors?

I quickly got out of bed and crept past my mother's bedroom door. It was barely open, and I could hear snoring coming from inside.

I put on some black clothes, packed my backpack with some old keys, a flashlight, milk, and Carpenter's Chewing Gum, and quietly left the house.

The theater looked like a sleeping elephant in the light cast by the street lamps. A light was on over the actors' entrance. Except for an iron door at the back of the building, all the entrances were secured with a deadbolt.

It was weird that this was the door that was left open. But for me, it was good luck. Very good luck.

My old keys were perfect for opening old-fashioned locks. The third key fit. Silently, I slipped into the building and closed the door behind me.

Then I switched on my flashlight. The narrow staircase to the basement was directly in front of me.

I climbed down the stairs and landed near the costumes. Soon, I was in front of the door that until now remained locked shut.

I shined the flashlight on the red door and noticed right away that it was locked with a deadbolt. The door must have been made out of heavy metal that probably wouldn't even open with the force of a hundred horses. But I wouldn't give up that quickly.

Luckily, Karl's workroom door was open. Except for a couple tissues, the pockets of his work shirt were completely empty. I didn't find anything on the shelves or in the drawers, either.

Suddenly, I noticed a cigar box on the workbench. It was filled to the brim with keys.

Sometimes, my job is boring. And sometimes, it's so exciting that I wouldn't trade it for anything in the world. This was a moment like that. I tried every single key in that deadbolt. On the twelfth try, it opened.

The room was smaller than any of the others in the basement. There was a big mirror on the wall and a big pile of clothing on the floor. I turned the beam of my flashlight to the heap . . . and what I saw on top of the pile was clearly a monster costume!

The scariest part of the costume was the rubber mask with long yellow teeth, eerie eyes, and creepy, mean eyebrows.

I took the costume and the mask under my arm and walked out of the room. I locked the door behind me, put the cigar box back in its place, and climbed back upstairs. Outside, thick clouds had covered the moon. I pulled the brim of my cap down to hide my face and made my way back home.

CHAPTER 5

Twelve Packs of Gum

At school the next day, I heard from Mrs. Linden that the next theater club rehearsal was going to take place during fifth and sixth periods. I asked her to ask Mr. Konzelmann to excuse me for those two hours.

When she asked whether I wanted to keep investigating, I just shrugged. I was sure of what I had seen, but giving away too much could be unlucky.

As the other kids used the actors' entrance, I entered the theater through the main entrance. The woman I thought was Mario's mother sat at the ticket booth and waited on a few customers.

I waited until she had to bend down to reach something. Then I crawled past her and went down to the basement.

Karl was sitting in his workroom, drinking coffee.

"You again?" he asked.

"I'll be done today," I answered.

"Do you need my help?" he asked.

I shook my head.

Karl was not going to get in my way. My plan would be completely ruined if he did.

After Karl got back to work, I quickly hid by the costumes. I put on the monster outfit.

On the way to the mountain of mattresses, I took a look in the mirror. I looked terrifying!

About five minutes later, I heard Mario's cue from onstage.

"Get out of here, you traitor!" cried Laura.

One second later, Mario plopped onto the mattresses. Quietly, I tiptoed over and tapped him on the shoulder.

I was expecting him to scream, to show how shocked he was. But that's not what happened.

Mario just turned around and said, "Quit it, Karl!"

Under my rubber mask, I smiled. With exactly three words, Mario had confessed.

With that, I ripped the mask from my face.

"K . . . K . . . Klooz?" Mario stuttered.

"Yes," I said.

"Oh, man," he murmured.

"It was a conspiracy," I said.

He nodded.

"Karl and your mom are involved. She's upstairs at the ticket booth, right?" I said.

He nodded.

"Karl played the monster so you could get the role," I said.

"Yes!" Mario cried. "But I really didn't want it! My mom wouldn't leave me alone. She thinks there should be at least one actor in the family."

Then two things happened at the same time. Mrs. Linden called for Mario from upstairs, and Karl started to realize that something wasn't right. As soon as he saw me in the monster costume, he turned about as pale as Mario.

"So what happens now?" he asked. "Are you going to call the cops?"

I shook my head.

"What's up, Mario?" Mrs. Linden called. "We're waiting for you!"

"Be here at four this afternoon," I said. "Then we'll see what happens."

* * *

When I came back to the theater that afternoon, Karl and Mario were already waiting for me. And they had brought someone with them: Mario's mom.

"Please don't tell on us, Klooz!" she cried. "Please! Karl and I will lose our jobs! And Mario won't be able to show his face in school!"

I stayed silent.

"Do you want money?" she asked. "Or tickets for theater shows?"

"I want Mario to give back the role," I answered.

"Is that it?" asked Karl.

"That's it," I said.

"And what should I tell Mrs. Linden?" Mario asked.

"Tell her that the role is too hard for you," I replied. "She'll believe you."

Mario looked at his mother. She nodded.

"And who's gonna take the role?" Karl wanted to know.

"That's my problem," I replied.

* * *

Greg was the best actor in school, and he deserved the lead role in the play.

That evening, I gave him a call and explained that Mario was giving him back the part.

I told him he didn't have to be afraid of the green monster anymore. I told him I gave the monster a swift kick in the pants, and it agreed to go away forever.

It didn't take Greg long to decide what to do. The next day, he said, he'd be at rehearsals.

The play was a great success. The applause never stopped. Most importantly, Greg and Laura got standing ovations.

I sat in the last row. I was really happy that everything was going so well.

On the way home, I saw Mario. "Hi, Klooz," he said.

"What's up, Mario?" I asked.

"I'm thinking of becoming a carpenter, and then I'll build sets for the theater," he told me.

"Good idea," I said.

Before we parted ways, he pressed something into my hand. When I opened it, I saw that there were five packs of Carpenter's Chewing Gum. "They're from Karl," he explained. "He says to say hi."

The next five packs were waiting for me at Olga's. "They're from Mrs. Linden," said my best friend. Then Olga passed two more packs across the counter toward me. "And these are from me," she explained. "My toothache is gone. The dentist pulled my wisdom tooth. Without you, I would have never gone."

So that was the story with the green monster in the theater basement. Maybe I should only work in the theater from now on. I've never earned so much chewing gum anywhere else.

The end

About the Author

Jürgen Banscherus is a worldwide phenomenon.
There are almost a million Klooz books in print, and
they have been translated into Spanish, Danish,
Thai, Chinese, and eleven other languages.
He has worked as a newspaper writer, a research
scientist, and a teacher. His first book for children
was published in 1985. He lives with his family in
Germany.

About the Illustrator

Ralf Butschkow was born in Berlin. He works as a
freelance graphic designer and illustrator, and has
published more than 50 books for children. Critics
have praised his work as "thoroughly enjoyable,"
"creatively original," and "highly recommended."

Glossary

anniversary (an-uh-VUR-suh-ree)—a date that people remember because something important happened on that date in the past

cashier (ka-SHIHR)—someone who takes money and gives tickets

conspiracy (kuhn-SPIHR-uh-see)—a secret plan by two or more people

deadbolt (DED-bohlt)—a lock

disappearance (diss-uh-PIHR-uhnss)—when someone goes out of sight

investigation (in-vess-tuh-GAY-shuhn)—finding out as much as possible about something

rehearsal (ri-HURSS-uhl)—a time to practice

role (ROHL)—the part that a person acts in a play

scene (SEEN)—a section of a play

solution (suh-LOO-shuhn)—the answer to a problem

suspicious (suh-SPISH-uhss)—acting as if they have done something wrong

Discussion Questions

1. How did Klooz solve this case?

2. Why did Mario, his mom, and Karl come up with the conspiracy? What else could they have done to make sure Mario got a good part in a play?

3. What do you think would be a good title for a play performed at your school's 100th-anniversary party?

Writing Prompts

1. Write a newspaper article that explains the events that happen in this book. Don't forget to include a headline.

2. Have you been in a play? Write about it. If you haven't, write about a play, movie, or TV show you would like to be in.

3. Pretend you're Mario. Write a letter to the other three actors, apologizing for scaring them.

More Klooz for

After School Ghost Hunter

If there aren't any ghosts, then what's that dark figure standing in the shadows?

Mystery Fans!

The Cheese Ball Trap

Klooz is on school break, and he's so bored that he'll even accept a case from his mother.